Dear mouse friends,
Welcome to the world of

Geronimo Stilton

The Editorial Staff of
The Rodent's Gazette

1. Linda Thinslice
2. Sweetie Cheesetriangle
3. Ratella Redfur
4. Soya Mousehao
5. Cheesita de la Pampa
6. Mouseanna Mousetti
7. Yale Youngmouse
8. Toni Tinypaw
9. Tina Spicytail
10. William Shortpaws
11. Valerie Vole
12. Trap Stilton
13. Branwen Musclemouse
14. Zeppola Zap
15. Merenguita Gingermouse
16. Ratsy O'Shea
17. Rodentrick Roundrat
18. Teddy von Muffler
19. Thea Stilton
20. Erronea Misprint
21. Pinky Pick
22. Ya-ya O'Cheddar
23. Mousella MacMouser
24. Kreamy O'Cheddar
25. Blasco Tabasco
26. Toffie Sugarsweet
27. Tylerat Truemouse
28. Larry Keys
29. Michael Mouse
30. Geronimo Stilton
31. Benjamin Stilton
32. Briette Finerat
33. Raclette Finerat

Geronimo Stilton
A learned and brainy
mouse; editor of
The Rodent's Gazette

Thea Stilton
Geronimo's sister and
special correspondent at
The Rodent's Gazette

Trap Stilton
An awful joker;
Geronimo's cousin and
owner of the store
Cheap Junk for Less

Benjamin Stilton
A sweet and loving
nine-year-old mouse;
Geronimo's favorite
nephew

Geronimo Stilton

THE TEMPLE OF
THE RUBY OF FIRE

Scholastic Inc.

New York   Toronto   London   Auckland   Sydney
Mexico City   New Delhi   Hong Kong   Buenos Aires

No part of this publication may be reproduced, stored in a retrieval system, or transmitted in any form or by any means, electronic, mechanical, photocopying, recording, or otherwise, without written permission from the copyright holder. For information regarding permission, please contact: Atlantyca S.p.A., Via Leopardi 8, 20123 Milan, Italy; e-mail foreignrights@atlantyca.it, www.atlantyca.com.

ISBN 978-0-439-66163-8

Based on an original idea by Elisabetta Dami.

www.geronimostilton.com

Published by Scholastic Inc., 557 Broadway, New York, NY 10012. SCHOLASTIC and associated logos are trademarks and/or registered trademarks of Scholastic Inc.

Stilton is the name of a famous English cheese. It is a registered trademark of the Stilton Cheese Makers' Association. For more information, go to www.stiltoncheese.com.

Text by Geronimo Stilton
Original title *Il tempio del rubino di fuoco*
Cover by Larry Keys
Illustrations by Johnny Stracchino and Mary Fontina
Graphics by Merenguita Gingermouse, Zeppola Zap, and Soya Mousehao

Special thanks to Kathryn Cristaldi
Translated by Joan L. Giurdanella
Interior design by Kay Petronio

36   18 19 20/0

Printed in the U.S.A.   40
First printing, December 2004

A MYSTERIOUS YELLOW ENVELOPE

Early one morning, I got up and ate breakfast. *Another day, another cheese danish,* I said to myself. Then I ran to the subway. I didn't want to be late for work.

Oops, I almost forgot to introduce myself. My name is Stilton, *Geronimo Stilton*. I run the most popular newspaper on Mouse Island. It's called *The Rodent's Gazette.*

Now wait, let's see, where was I . . . oh, yes, I was on my way to the office. When I got there, I found a mysterious

Geronimo Stilton

yellow envelope on my desk. It was addressed to me. I recognized the handwriting. It belonged to Professor Paws von Volt.

The professor was a famous scientist. We became friends during one of my many adventures.

I slit open the envelope. My paws were trembling with excitement.

Any message from the professor is always thrilling. But it wasn't a message that thrilled me this time. It was four plane tickets to CLUB MOUSE in Crocodilia.

Mr. Geronimo Stilton
Publisher, The Rodent's Gazette
17 Swiss Cheese Center
New Mouse City, Mouse Island
13131

Do you know where Crocodilia is? It is on the Amazon River in Brazil!

The tickets were made out to me; my nephew Benjamin; my sister, Thea; and my cousin Trap. I *wondered* why the professor needed our help in the Amazon. It was all very mysterious.

I called my sister. She is the special correspondent for *The Rodent's Gazette.* "Hold on to your whiskers! I have incredible news!" I announced. "Professor von Volt has sent us tickets to join him on the Amazon!"

My sister squeaked so loud, my ears rang. "HOLEY CHEESE! What a fabumouse scoop for *The Rodent's Gazette!*" she cried. "You get the gear. I'll tell the others. We'll meet at the airport in fifteen minutes."

One thing you should know about my sister. She LOVES to give orders.

MY EARS ARE NOT STUFFED WITH CHEESE!

I *RAN* right away to Rats Authority, the best store in town for sporting goods. I picked up some stuff for our trip to the tropics. Then I *RUSHED* to the airport.

My little nephew Benjamin gave me a mouse-sized hug. "Uncle Geronimo, I'm so glad I'm going with you!" he squeaked.

I smiled. Oh, how I love that nephew of mine.

Oh, how I love him.

Just then, my sister started yelling at me.

My little nephew Benjamin

"Did you get everything, **Gerry Berry?** Well? Well?" she demanded.

When I didn't answer right away, she pinched my tail. "Are your ears stuffed with cheese, Geronimoid?" she added.

Did I mention my sister can be a pain in my fur?

Thea popped open my suitcase. Then she began DIGGING THROUGH IT.

I had packed four pairs of waterproof knee-high boots, four pairs of comfy CAMOUFLAGE pants, four hats with mosquito netting, a first-aid kit, and more. "Looks like you have everything," Thea said approvingly.

But right then, a voice chimed in. "Everything? Are you kidding?" it scoffed. "If it weren't for me you would have forgotten the most important thing... **food!**"

I turned around, but I knew already who was squeaking. It was my cousin Trap. That mouse could eat a five-hundred-pound rodent under the table. Yes, eating was not

My sister, Thea, the special correspondent for *The Rodent's Gazette*

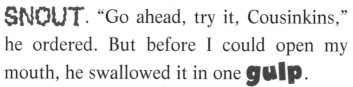

just a hobby for Trap. It was his life!

Now he WAVED a piece of Swiss cheese under my SNOUT. "Go ahead, try it, Cousinkins," he ordered. But before I could open my mouth, he swallowed it in one **gulp**.

I was furious.

"Ha-ha-ha! You always fall for it, Germeister!" Trap guffawed.

Then he showed me a little silver knife he wore around his neck. "I just finished a cheese-tasting course," he explained. "I always wear this little knife around my neck. You never know when something yummy may pass your way."

Suddenly, a big, **BEEFY** rodent in a muscle T-shirt walked by. He was munching on a cheddar sandwich. Trap took one look at that sandwich and whipped out his knife. Before I could stop him, he'd sliced off a **PIECE** of it!

Muscle Mouse turned around. He was infuriated. And he was glaring right at me. "Hey, you! What do you think you're doing?" he shrieked.

I tried to explain, but he wouldn't listen.

"If I catch you, I will tie your tail into knots!" he shouted, chasing after me.

I hid in the restroom.

Cheese niblets!

This trip was getting off to a

terrible start!

If I Catch You, I Will Rearrange Your Fur!

FIVE hours later, the plane was ready to take off. I was still hiding in the restroom. What else could I do? I didn't want to get mashed to a pulp by old Muscle Mouse. I could hear him squeaking outside the door.

"If I catch that rotten mouse, I'll twist off his tail! I'll rearrange his fur!" he growled.

My teeth were chattering so fast, they could have won a tap dancing contest. I waited until the last possible moment to leave the restroom.

"Last call for flight 285 departing for Crocodilia! Last call!" a voice announced.

This was it. I had to make a **BREAK** for it. Quiet as a mouse, I slipped out of the restroom. Then I **RACED** for the plane.

Paws pounded after me. "Come back here, you no-good cheese nibbler!" I heard Muscle Mouse screech.

With one last gasp, I jumped onboard. A few minutes later, we took off.

The trip was very long. After all, the Amazon River is not on Mouse Island. It is far, far away in South America. That's a whole other continent!

Crocodilia

Amazon River

South America

BIG-TIME FUN!

Finally, we arrived. A **tall, lanky** mouse with red shorts, curly fur, and a **purple** ponytail greeted us.

"Welcome to Club Mouse!" he yelled. "Are you ready for some big-time fun? We've got big-time volleyball! We've got big-time water polo! You name it, we've got it — *big-time!*" He was jumping up and down like an aerobics instructor.

I rolled my eyes. Oh, how I hate these types of resorts. I'm not into organized activities. I just like to do my own thing. I couldn't wait for the professor to show up.

Then I noticed Ponytail Mouse was staring at me. "You need to turn that pout inside out, Stilton. *Big-time!*" he said.

Before I could stop him, he began tickling the bottom of my paws. I rolled on the ground in a fit of giggles. Can you guess why? I am very ticklish!

"Excellent! Now you've got it, Stilton!" Ponytail Mouse shrieked.

Then he waved his tail in the air. "THEME SONG!" he called out.

Five sweaty mice appeared out of nowhere. They began to dance and sing.

Rowdyrat Bigtime

Ha-ha-ha!

"Here at the club we're into big-time fun,
We like to swim and dance and sing,
We like to do most anything.
So join on in now, don't be shy,
Give snorkeling a big-time try.
Yes, at Club Mouse we never frown,
And if you do, we'll track you down!"

When the song ended, Ponytail Mouse clapped his paws. "Hello, rodents and gentlemice!" he yelled. "I am the head of this club! My name is **Rowdyrat Bigtime!** I'd like to remind you that our

Boom chicka boom-boom!

HEE-HEE HA-HA lessons start at six o'clock!"

Hee-hee ha-ha lessons? What were they? Probably some ridiculous Club Mouse ritual. I shook my head. Did I tell you I hate organized activities? I glanced at my watch. It was exactly six o'clock on the snout.

Just then, Rowdyrat grabbed me by the tail. Slimy Swiss balls! He was dragging me up to a big stage.

I turned pale. I hate dancing. I hate singing. But most of all, I hate making a fool of myself.

"Let me go, PLEASE!" I squeaked.

But Rowdyrat didn't listen. He forced me to dance. The crowd roared with laughter.

Then Rowdyrat tickled the bottom of my paws.

I rolled around in the sand in a fit of giggles. Oh, why did I have to be so ticklish?

"Stilton, you're going to have big-time fun

even if it kills you!" Rowdyrat insisted.

I groaned . . . *big-time.*

Meanwhile, Rowdyrat was busy making more announcements. "I love you all, Club Mousers!" he yelled to the crowd. Everyone cheered. "And now it's time for our **water polo tournament**!" he continued. "Last one in the pool is a rotten rodent!"

The crowd made a mad dash for the water. I made a mad dash for my room. I'd had enough of this big-time nonsense. Enough to last a lifetime! I couldn't wait for Professor von Volt to arrive.

"And now it's time for our water polo tournament! Last one in the pool is a rotten rodent!"

THESE ARE CALLED CLICK-CLICKS!

Ten minutes later, Benjamin skipped into my room. A huge grin spread across his face. "Uncle, look! I caught a crab," he squeaked happily.

He held out a disgusting ORANGE crab that had a ferocious look.

My fur stood on end. "Wh-where did you find it?" I stammered.

Benjamin pointed outside. "Right here, on the beach. **Rowdyrat Bigtime** taught me how to fish for crabs," he explained. "He said these are called click-clicks. I don't know why, though."

I started to tell him to put the crab down when

CLICK-CLICK
CLICK-CLICK
CLICK-CLICK

tragedy struck. First that HIDEOUS creature glared at me. Then it jumped at me and pinched my tail with its claws. CLICK-CLICK!

"Ow! Ow! Owwwwwwwwwwwwwwwwwwwwwwwwwwwwwwwwwwww!"

I shrieked at the top of my lungs.

"Uncle, are you OK?" Benjamin cried.

I didn't want to alarm my nephew. "Let me explain to you why they call it a click-click," I mumbled. Then I *fainted*.

WHEN IN DOUBT, I GIVE AN INJECTION

I came to in the infirmary. "What . . . where am I . . . the crab . . . click-click . . . " I babbled.

Dr. Wacky Whiskers held up a long, pointy needle. "When in doubt, I give an injection," he said. "Everything gets better with an injection."

My eyes nearly popped out of my fur. *Quick as a flash, I jumped out of bed.*

I raced for the door, screaming, "It's a miracle! I'm cured!"

Oh, when was Professor von Volt going to get here?

I found Benjamin in our room. *"Uncle, how do you feel?"* he asked.

Dr. Wacky Whiskers

Just then, Rowdyrat poked his snout in the door. He tried to tickle me. I bounced into the **AIR** . . . and landed on a sea urchin. "Yowee!" I shrieked.

"Uncle, I'm so sorry," my nephew apologized. "Rowdyrat helped me find that sea urchin on the beach."

I should have known. That obnoxious rodent was getting to be a big-time pain in my fur!

They carried me to the infirmary on a stretcher.

Dr. Wacky Whiskers shook his head. "You again, Stilton?" he mumbled. He grasped a syringe. "When in doubt, I give an injection. Everything gets better with an injection!" he declared.

This time, I didn't have the strength to run. **Oh, how did I get myself into such a mess?!**

I bounced off the bed and into the air.

WORSE THAN TUTANKHAMEN'S MUMMY

Thea and Trap came to see me in the infirmary.

"This place is great!" Thea squeaked. "I'm enjoying myself *big-time*. Today, I took aerobics, *windsurfing*, water-skiing, **KICKBOXING**, and deep-sea diving lessons!"

Trap nodded. "I'm having the best time, too!" he agreed. "I played *big-time* soccer with Rowdyrat. Then I stuffed myself *big-time* at the Chuckle Cheese Hut."

Thea enjoying herself windsurfing!

"Sounds great," I mumbled. But I was lying. I'm not much of a sportsmouse. And who knows what kind of cheap food they serve at a place called the Chuckle Cheese Hut.

As soon as I felt better, I decided to go to the beach with Benjamin.

Trap stuffing himself!

I dipped my paw in the water. Brrr! It was cold. Maybe I'd stick to sunbathing.

Just then, a mouse came racing right for me. He was screaming something.

I groaned. It was Rowdyrat. I dove into the water to get away from him.

That's when I found myself in the middle

of a **SCHOOL OF JELLYFISH!** They **STUNG** me all over — even on the tail! Rats! Rowdyrat pulled me out of the water. "I was trying to warn you that there are big-time jellyfish in there," he said.

Dr. Wacky Whiskers shook his head when he saw me. "Stilton. What a surprise," he smirked.

He smeared a disgusting, **STINKY** cream all over my fur. Then he wrapped me up in bandages. I was more preserved than Tutankhamen's mummy!

"When in doubt, I like to give an injection," the

doctor told me. As if I didn't know that already. He pulled out his long needle.

I was horrified. I was queasy. I was never so glad to see my cousin Trap in all my life. He **WHISKED** me away in a wheelbarrow before old Wacky Whiskers could stick me again.

Oh, I couldn't wait for Professor von Volt to arrive.

WOULD YOU PREFER WIND, STENCH, OR MOSQUITOES?

Wind

The next morning, Benjamin and I went to the beach. I stretched out on the sand with my book, *Inspector Cheesy Cracks the Case.* I love reading silly mysteries when I'm on vacation.

Ah, now this was the life. The sun, the sand, the surf . . . the **WIND** ?? Yes, the wind was so strong, it nearly ripped my whiskers off! **Rats**!

I packed up my things. We moved to another beach. Yes, this was more like it.

No wind on this beach. But what was that awful smell? I grabbed my nose. The **STENCH** was worse than my cousin Stinkyfur after a workout. **¡it stinks!**

Once again, we moved to another beach. Cheese niblets! This one was infested with mosquitoes.

Oh, where was the professor? This place was a **NIGHTMARE!**

Benjamin tried to cheer me up. "Uncle, don't be upset. It's not so bad," he soothed.

"What do you prefer — the wind, the stench, or the mosquitoes?"

Before I could answer, a seagull began

circling overhead. "SQUAWK! SQUAWK!"

I shuddered. I don't trust seagulls. One time, a seagull stole my glasses right off my face. It took me ten hours to find my way back to my beach blanket.

Just then, the seagull dropped something on my head. It was a piece of paper wrapped around a heavy wrench.

"HOLEY CHEESE!" I squeaked.

Benjamin read the note out loud:

> *Dear Friend,*
> *I knew I could count on you. I will wait for you at midnight down by the river. Make sure nobody sees you. It is very important we keep our meeting a secret.*
> *Mousey regards,*
> *Professor Paws von Volt*

I breathed a SIGH OF RELIEF. Finally, the professor had arrived!

LAND, SEA, OR SKY?

At **MIDNIGHT**, Thea, Trap, Benjamin, and I went to the river. How would the professor get there? By **land**, by SEA, or by sky?

You see, the professor liked to use many different types of transportation — trucks, helicopters, submarines. They were all made in his laboratory. Every one ran on solar energy. He was always perfecting them. One day, the professor wanted to pass on his inventions to the world. A planet without any pollution was his **BIGGEST DREAM**.

I paced up and down the riverbank. Benjamin stuck to my side like glue. "Tell me

solar energy solar energy solar energy

again, Uncle, about the time you saw the professor on Mouse Everest. That must have been so cool," he squeaked. "I wonder if I could be the professor's assistant while we're here. Can you ask him, Uncle? Can you? Can you?"

I nodded. The professor had never met Benjamin, but I knew he would love him. Who wouldn't love such a sweet, adorable mouse?

Suddenly, the water began foaming with waves. A yellow submarine decorated with cheese holes broke the surface.

With a loud POP! the hatch opened. A pair of mouse ears stuck out.

"Professor von Volt!" I called.

"*Stilton, Geronimo Stilton!*" the professor answered. "Welcome, my friend!"

A yellow submarine decorated with cheese holes broke the surface.

THE IMPORTANCE OF BEING STILTON

The professor invited us inside his submarine, the *Vonderwater*. He explained how the sub ran on batteries. "The top part of the submarine is made up of silicon crystals," he said. "When the CRYSTALS are exposed to **sunlight**, the batteries are instantly recharged!"

The professor led us into a huge living room. A Steinrat grand piano stood in the corner. I wished I could play. But I wasn't a very musical mouse. I had trouble playing the kazoo. Behind the piano was a bookcase filled with books. On the walls hung the professor's beloved collection of priceless paintings.

Besides the living room, there was a kitchen, an aquarium, a greenhouse for growing fruits and vegetables, and a computer room.

"Holey cheese! This place has everything!" I **remarked**.

The professor patted my shoulder with his paw. "Yes, everything, except a good friend," he said with a **grin**. "You are a true *gentlemouse*, Geronimo Stilton."

I blushed. But I noticed Trap rolling his eyes. He hates it when rodents talk sappy. "So, do you have anything to eat?" he asked, patting his tummy.

I groaned. Oh, why was I related to such an *obnoxious* mouse?

PROFESSOR PAWS VON VOLT

The "Vonderwater," Professor Paws von Volt's submarine

1. Silicon crystals that absorb solar energy
2. Command room with turret
3. Periscope
4. Watertight door
5. Computer room
6. Machine room
7. Kitchen
8. Boiler room
9. Bathroom

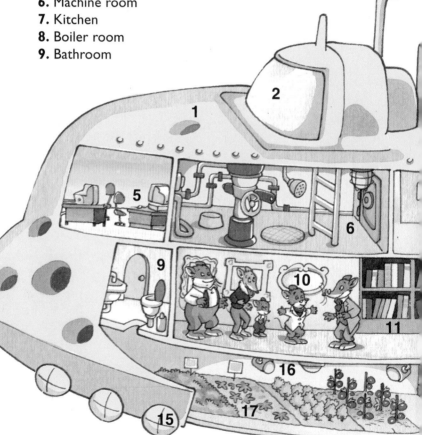

10. Art collection
11. Library
12. Piano
13. Desalinization equipment
14. Electrical center
15. Underwater camera
16. Solar lamps
17. Planting beds
18. Aquarium
19. Motors and turbines
20. Screw propellers

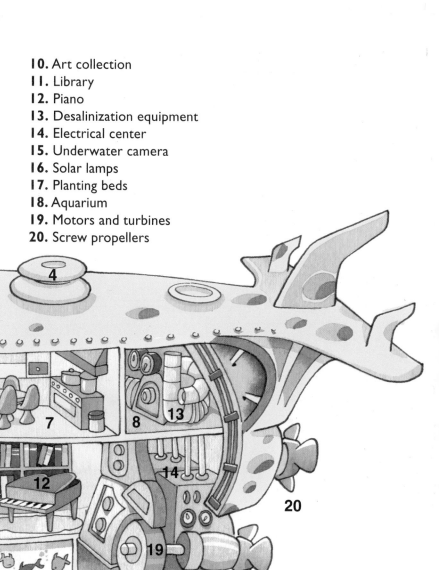

This submarine is powered by nonpolluting solar energy.

The professor offered us a plate of cheese sandwiches. Then he told us why he had brought us to the Amazon. "I am searching for an ancient Incan temple," he began. "It is said to be hidden in the thick trees and plants next to the river. Inside the temple is a giant **ruby**. It would be an amazing archaeological find. I thought you might like to join me."

We all agreed enthusiastically.

"Wait till they hear about this at school!" Benjamin squeaked. I told the professor how my nephew wanted to be his assistant.

Volt beamed. "That would be fabumouse," he cried. "I really need a trusty rodent to take notes for me."

Benjamin was *thrilled*. "Thanks, Professor, you won't be sorry!" he exclaimed, giving me a hug.

A Voyage on the Amazon River

Soon we were on our way. We sailed up the Amazon River. What an UNBELIEVABLE sight! The plants were lush and incredibly green. Multicolored birds sat on the branches of the trees. Crocodiles floated like killer logs in the water. Enormouse hairy spiders, carnivorous ants, and poisonous snakes watched us from the shore. I shivered. I was glad I was on the sub. Don't get me wrong, I like WILDLIFE as much as the next rodent. But this wildlife was a little TOO wild, if you know what I mean.

I chewed my whiskers to keep from shrieking with fear. I didn't want anyone to call me a scaredy mouse. I forced

myself to listen to the professor. He was giving Benjamin a history lesson.

"The first European rodent to land in the Americas was Christopher Columouse in 1492. But he thought he had reached INDIA. That's why he called the local people Indians. After Columouse, the conquistadors arrived from Spain. They were soldiers who conquered land in the

name of the king of Spain.
Next, ADVENTURERS
from Portugal came. They
colonized Brazil," he explained.

"Why is the river called the Amazon
River?" Benjamin asked.

"Perhaps some of the soldiers saw native
women sailing up the river, armed with bows
and arrows. These FIGHTING women
made them think of the Amazon warriors in
Greek *mythology*," the professor suggested.

Then the professor sighed deeply. He said he was worried about the Amazon Forest.

Long ago, the conquistadors had destroyed lots of historic artifacts. They had forced the natives to give up their traditions.

Today, greedy mice continue to damage the forest. They chop down trees and pollute the water. "If it doesn't stop **SOON**, we will have an ecological **DISASTER** on our paws," the professor moaned, shaking his head sadly.

Along the river, we noticed huts made out of leaves. Natives armed with bows and arrows peeked out. When they saw the professor, they smiled and *RAN* down to the river.

"These are the Yanomami. Like their ancestors, they live in the forest. The forest provides them with everything they need to survive," the professor explained. "They love nature and they respect it. We should all follow their example."

He docked the submarine. Then he *embraced* their chief. You could see that they were great friends!

THE YANOMAMI

We stayed with the Yanomami for a few days. We listened to stories around the *FIRE*. A Yanomami taught Benjamin how to make *bracelets* out of toucan feathers. Another painted designs on Thea's fur with sap from urucu berries. "I can't wait to show Timmy Tidytail at the salon," my sister gushed.

Yes, those Yanomami were fascinating rodents. I could write all about them in *The Rodent's Gazette*.

The chief explained how worried he was about the forest being cut down.

I nodded.

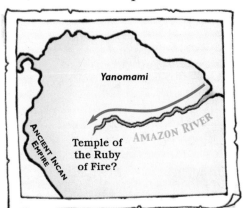

Maybe I could write about that, too. "I will try to help you," I promised the chief.

Soon it was time to go. We said good-bye to our new friends. Then we sailed up the river.

YANOMAMI

Today, around 32,000 Yanomami live in the Amazon. Their first sustained contact with western civilization came in the 1940s and 50s. In the 1980s, gold was discovered in their land and it was invaded by miners. The miners polluted the rivers and destroyed the forest to build roads.

A Mysterious Noise

Soon we reached the beginning of the Amazon River. We were in the land of the legendary Incan empire!

The professor turned on the COMPUTER. He showed us a bird's-eye view of the forest.

"The plants are less dense here," he said, pointing to a spot. "I think that's where we should search for the *TEMPLE OF THE RUBY OF FIRE*."

We hid the submarine in a cove on the river. Then we trudged through the forest.

We walked for hours, cutting through the vines with machetes.

I was sweating. My back was aching. And I had blisters all over my paws. Rats! I couldn't wait to get back home. I would book a whole day at the *Restful Rodent*. Have you ever been there? It's one of the most relaxing spas in New Mouse City.

Finally, we reached a tiny village.

The chief greeted us warmly. "Welcome, strangers. My name is Strongfur. This is my wife, Warmfur. And this is my daughter, Monkeyfur," he said. "Please, follow me, and I will introduce you to the rest of our village."

That night, we sat together around the FIRE. The chief and his family were warm and friendly. *I could get used to this place,* I decided. It would be great to escape the rat race. Maybe I could even change my name. Brainyfur might work. Or maybe Trustyfur.

I was still thinking about a good name for

Warmfur

Strongfur

Monkeyfur

myself when the chief's wife asked, "What brings you all so far from home?"

"We are looking for the Temple of the Ruby of Fire," Professor von Volt said.

Strongfur jumped to his paws. He had a strange look on his face. "There is no temple. There is no ruby," he said. "YOU MUST GIVE UP YOUR SEARCH!"

The whole village repeated his words. "No temple! No ruby! No search!"

We were shocked. What were the villagers hiding? Still, something told us not to argue. For once, even my obnoxious cousin kept his snout shut.

That night, I was snoring happily when a mysterious noise woke me up.

"What was that?" Thea whispered.

It sounded like something buzzing.

WATCH OUT FOR THE BITERS!

The next morning, we asked the chief about the strange noise.

"Noise? What noise?" he answered.

"Noise? What noise?" the natives repeated.

Deep in thought, I went to the river to get washed. I bumped into the chief's daughter, Monkeyfur.

"Watch out for the Biters. There are a lot of them in the river," she advised.

I looked into the crystal-blue water. I didn't see anything. I wondered what she was talking about. So I bent over to wash my face.

Suddenly, Monkeyfur began jumping up and

down. "Biters! **Watch out!**" she squeaked.

She pointed to a school of fish headed for me.

They were so small and colorful. "Oh, those cute little fish won't hurt you. Here, fishy, fishy!" I said, sticking my paw out. I grinned at Monkeyfur. She needed to get out more. Maybe I could help her overcome her fear of fish. Even a scaredy mouse like myself had overcome my fear of the **dark**.

YIKES!

Well, sort of. I still slept with my Cheeseball the Clown night-light on. But don't tell anyone.

Just then, I noticed something odd. The fish had opened their jaws. I saw two rows of teeth. Sharp teeth! Rancid rat hairs! Now I knew what Biters were. They were piranhas!

I jumped out of the river in three leaps.

Monkeyfur breathed a SIGH of relief.

My paws were shaking like furry leaves. I decided to rest under a tree.

But before I could sit down, Monkeyfur began screaming again.

"WATCH OUT FOR THE CAIMAN!,"

she yelped.

HELPPPPPPP!!!!!!!!!

CLICK!

I jumped up. **CLICK!** An enormouse CROCODILE snapped his jaws at me.

I headed back to the village. "Watch out for the **TAIL-THAT-STINGS** and the VINE-THAT-SUFFOCATES!" Monkeyfur called.

I looked all around.

I saw nothing.

Nothing at all.

Was Monkeyfur pulling my tail?

"You are looking, but you are not seeing,"

Monkeyfur explained. She pointed to a poisonous black scorpion HIDDEN in the leaves. Then she showed me an ANACONDA SLITHERING ON A BRANCH RIGHT OVER MY HEAD!

Cheese niblets!

Monkeyfur giggled. "If you want to survive in the forest, you need to use your eyes better," she advised.

I nodded. "You saved my life. How can I *thank* you?" I asked.

"C" Like in Caiman

Monkeyfur showed me a notebook. "Do you know how to **read**?" she asked.

When I nodded, she looked impressed. It seemed no one in the village knew how to **read** or write. Can you imagine? **Reading** and writing are my life!

"Only *THEY* can do it," Monkeyfur blurted out. Then she clamped a paw over her mouth.

"Who are *they*?" I asked. But she wasn't squeaking. I was dying to know what secret Monkeyfur was keeping. But I decided it wouldn't be right to pry. After all, she had just saved my life. Instead, I offered to teach her how to **read** and write.

We sat down by the riverbank. We began

with the alphabet. " *'A' like in apple, 'B' like in banana,*" I recited.

Monkeyfur giggled. "I think I've got it," she said. Then she pointed to a pair of yellow eyes watching us from the river. " *'C' like in caiman,*" she said. She grabbed my paw, and we raced back to the village.

Yes, Monkeyfur was a fast learner. But I was the fastest runner with that croc on our tails!

In the Dead
of Night

That **NIGHT**, I went to sleep with my clothes on. I put my flashlight next to my sleeping bag. I wasn't taking any chances. What if a snake slithered under the door? What if a scorpion crawled through the window? What if my cousin put **ITCHING POWDER** in my sleeping bag? Trap loves to play pranks on me. Once he tied a bell to my tail. When I took a step, I sounded just like a cheese ice cream truck. Rodents came running from all over town!

I was sleeping soundly when I was woken up by a noise. It was the same **MYSTERIOUS** noise from the night before.

I woke up Thea, Trap, Benjamin, and

*A team of rodents was busy
cutting down trees.*

Professor von Volt. Quiet as mice, we went to investigate.

We discovered a horrifying scene. A team of rodents was busy **cutting down** trees. They put the trees on a ▩▩▩ ▩▩▩▩▩. Soon there would be no trees left!

The professor was furious. *"Scoundrels!"* he whispered, enraged. "They have no respect for the forest!"

We decided we'd better keep quiet. I mean, these were rotten rodents. Rotten to the core.

One chubby mouse appeared to be the boss. The others called him **Nastytail**. His fur

Nastytail

was slicked back on his head. He wore a huge gold medal around his neck. It said, I'M NASTY — AND PROUD OF IT! He had a **thick** gold watch on his wrist. A glittering diamond hung from his ear.

"Bones, do this! Bones, do that!" he shrieked at a mouse as thin as string cheese. The mouse was wearing a black shirt decorated with skeleton heads. He had an evil expression on his snout. I shivered.

"OK, Boss, we're done here," he told Nastytail. "Tomorrow **NIGHT** we'll change campsites. But we'd better watch out for those natives. We don't want them getting any funny ideas."

BONES

Just then, an enormouse rodent with a crewcut came strutting over. His paws were as big as my aunt Ratilda's ten-pound cheddar logs. His teeth looked like they were made out of steel. His name was **MIKE MICESON**.

"Don't worry, I'll handle them," he sneered, grinning at Nastytail. "If they get out of line, I'll just squash 'em!"

He jumped up and down, punching the air. Then he punched a tree. It split in two. Part of the trunk fell on his foot. A big hairy spider crawled out of the trunk and bit his toe.

MIKE MICESON

"OWWWWWWWWWWWWWWWWWWWWWWWWWWWWWWW!"

the big mouse screamed.

Bones giggled under his whiskers.

Nastytail just rolled his eyes. "Miceson!" he squeaked. "You may be big, but you have the brain of a BUG!"

THE STRANGERS ARE RIGHT!

The next morning, I talked to Strongfur. "We know about the evil rodents who are destroying your forest," I said. "We want to help. We must stop them before it's too late."

Strongfur shook his head sadly. "I'm afraid no one can help," he said with a sigh. "**They** have threatened to **BURN** down our homes."

Suddenly, Monkeyfur jumped to her paws. "The strangers are right!" she cried. "We must return to the **HOUSE OF THE HOWLING SPIRITS**, where the tombs of our ancestors are buried!"

"Howling Spirits?" muttered Thea.

"Tombs?" added Benjamin.

"Okay, spill the beans," said Trap.

Slowly, Strongfur let us in on their secret. It seems they were the last descendants of the Incas. For years, they had been living deep in the forest next to the House of the Howling Spirits. It was the same as the place we called the **TEMPLE OF THE RUBY OF FIRE**. Then the **EVIL RODENTS** had come and began chopping down trees. Strongfur and the rest of the villagers were driven away.

I watched Monkeyfur listening to her father. She looked angry. "Father, please let me go with the strangers," she pleaded. "Together we will stop the evil ones. We should not have to live in fear."

After a few minutes, Strongfur nodded. He hugged his daughter. "You may go," he agreed. *"But remember, you must be sly like a monkey."*

THE HOUSE OF THE HOWLING SPIRITS

We decided to leave in the **MIDDLE OF THE NIGHT**. We crept on tippy paws out of our hut. Monkeyfur met us on the **PATH**. She led us deep into the forest.

Even though it was nighttime, it was **HOT**. Terribly hot. Sweat dripped off my tail. And my whiskers. And my eyelashes. **Cheese niblets!** I felt like I was locked in the sauna at the Muscle Mouse. Have you ever been there? It's a popular health club in New Mouse City. I went in once just to check it out. I got my tail stuck in the treadmill. I dropped a pink dumbbell on my paw. Then I fell off the bicycle. How embarrassing! Oh, well. You may have

already guessed, I'm not very athletic.

I was getting to be a good observer, though. Monkeyfur had taught me how.

A jaguar is hidden in this picture. Can you find it?

I looked around. I saw all of the details I had never noticed before. I saw an insect hidden in a flower. I saw a snake underneath a mossy TREE trunk. I saw a caiman sunk into the MUD. I pulled Benjamin aside. I showed him all of these things. Now he, too, could learn the difference between looking and seeing.

In the meantime, Thea was busy snapping pictures right and left. Trap tried to get in all of her shots. "Cheese!" he squeaked,

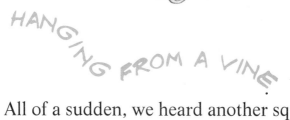

HANGING FROM A VINE

All of a sudden, we heard another squeak. No, it wasn't really a squeak. It was more like a scream. "Wh-wh-wh-at is th-th-th-at?" I stammered.

Monkeyfur motioned for us to stay quiet. "That is the scream of the **HOWLING SPIRITS**. We must be close to their house," she whispered.

A praying mantis is hidden in this picture. Can you find it?

I gulped. I was scared silly. I mean, who wants to meet a bunch of spirits? Especially howling ones. I wondered what they were howling about. Maybe they were hungry. Maybe they were cold. Or maybe they wanted to scare us living rodents to death. Then they'd take over our bodies, move into our homes, and rearrange our furniture. What a NIGHTMARE!

Oh, how I hate these scary adventures!

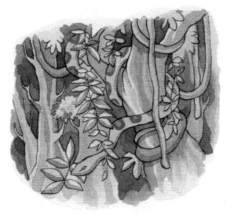

An anaconda is hidden in this picture. Can you find it?

WHO DO I HAVE TO SQUASH, BOSS?

I pulled out my binoculars with shaky paws. I could see Nastytail's campsite. Then I saw something else. Hidden in the vegetation was a stone structure covered with vines.

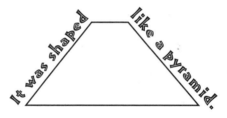

It was shaped like a pyramid.

The only thing missing was a point at the top.

All around the structure were tall columns of stone. It was the remains of an ancient Incan village! Professor von Volt was so excited, he nearly squeaked with joy. Luckily, Trap put a paw over his mouth before he blew our cover.

This is where our ancestors lived.

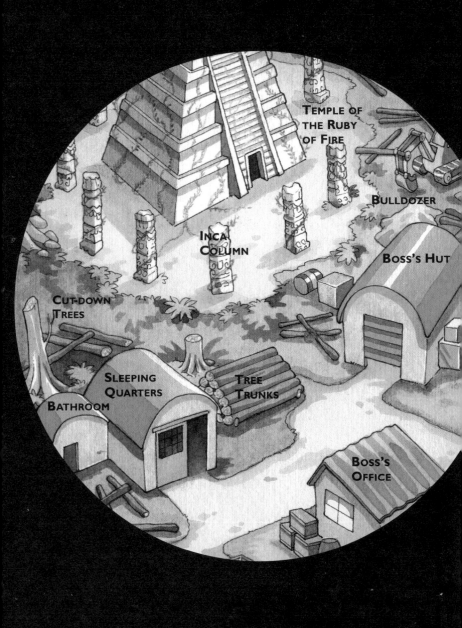

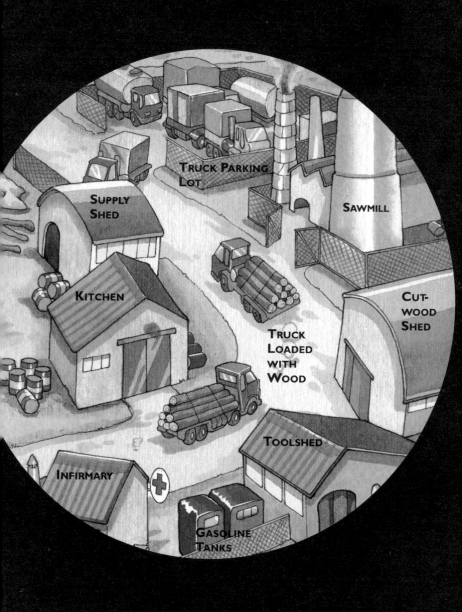

"This is where our ancestors lived," Monkeyfur whispered. "We lived here, too, until the EVIL ONES arrived."

We crept nearer. The **shadows** kept us well hidden.

We listened as Nastytail barked out orders. "Tomorrow, we will cut down all the trees surrounding the temple," he said. "Those trees are very valuable. Soon we will be rolling in cheese. But we need to speed up the work. I want it all gone by the end of the day!"

Bones chewed his whiskers. "Um, but what about Strongfur and the natives, Boss?" he asked. "What will they do?"

Nastytail let out an evil laugh. I guess they didn't call him Nastytail for nothing.

Miceson stood up and began punching the air. "I'll tell them what to do, Boss," he sniggered. "Just tell me who to SQUASH and I'll SQUASH 'em!"

He danced around in a circle like a boxing champion. Then he tripped over a log. He landed on a pile of red earth. It was a termite nest!

Miceson ran to the stream, screaming. Bones was giggling under his whiskers.

Nastytail shook his head. "Such a big fool." He sighed.

AAAAAAAAAAGHHHHHHHH!

But Where Is the Ruby?

An hour later, Nastytail and his crew were sound asleep.

We headed for the **_Temple of the Ruby of Fire_**.

Monkeyfur led the way inside. Flickering **candles** hanging on the walls cast eerie shadows all around. My heart was racing as fast as my uncle Cheesebelly at an All-U-Can-Eat cheddar buffet.

Suddenly, we heard a bloodcurdling **SCREAM**.

"Do not worry. Those are just the Howling Spirits," Monkeyfur explained.

Just the Howling Spirits? I felt like I was

about to faint. Oh, how I wished I were home in my safe, comfy mouse hole!

But before I could pass out, I saw something. No, not just one something. A whole lot of somethings! A bunch of black monkeys were swinging from the beams above our heads. They were howling at the top of their lungs.

Just then, they spotted Monkeyfur. They came down to greet her.

She spoke to them in a strange language. "Ooo! Ooo! Eee! Eee!" The monkeys answered her with a big group hug.

"See, they will not hurt you," Monkeyfur told us. "They are my friends."

Professor von Volt was busy studying the temple. He dictated some notes to his new assistant, Benjamin.

I looked around. In the main room there was a large, round well. A big, dusty stone covered the well.

"This is where I used to place the fruit for the Howling Spirits to eat," Monkeyfur said. "It was once a SACRIFICIAL ALTAR."

Thea snapped away with her camera. The temple was fascinating. There were strange inscriptions on the walls in the hallway. And drawings of all types of animals and plants. I felt like I was back in the time of the Incas.

"But where is the RUBY?" Trap asked Monkeyfur.

INCAS

The Incas lived in Peru since 1500 B.C. Until the end of the fifteenth century, their empire included Ecuador, Peru, Bolivia, Chile, and parts of Argentina.

In 1532, the Incan king Atahualpa was captured by the Spanish conquistador Francisco Pizarro, who took over the kingdom. The Spaniards destroyed the Incan treasures, which had immeasurable artistic and historic value. They melted the Incas' gold and burned their artifacts.

A COLUMN OF FIRE

Monkeyfur grinned. Then she pointed to the dusty stone covering the well.

Trap wiped some of the dust off the stone. Then Thea took one of the torches off the wall and held it over the stone.

"Well, I'll be a rodent's uncle!" Trap shouted. The stone sparkled in the light. We had found the RUBY OF FIRE!

"This stone hides a secret," Monkeyfur said. She told us the stone worked like a faucet. When you turned it, precious drops of the Oil of Fire came out. The villagers had been using the oil to light their lamps for centuries.

I turned the ruby slowly. A few drops of

TURNING TURNING TURNING TURNING

THE TEMPLE OF THE RUBY OF FIRE

1. Torches on the walls
2. Fresco
3. Sacrificial altar
4. Ruby covering the well
5. Well
6. Monkey-shaped faucet
7. Empty terra-cotta jugs
8. Table where the fruit is placed for the monkeys
9. Entrance

DARK LIQUID dripped out.

"Let me try that, Germeister," my cousin insisted. He pushed me aside. Then he yanked on the ruby full force.

"Stop!" everyone screamed. But it was too late. A huge spray of oil gushed out.

THIS IS HOW IT WORKS:
When you twist gently, a tiny bit at a time, the Ruby makes the monkey-shaped faucet produce a few drops of oil.

A spark from Thea's torch made the oil burst into flames. The well became a column of **fire**!

We didn't know what to do. We couldn't exactly call 911. But luckily Monkeyfur came to our rescue. She slammed the big stone over the fire. The flames died down all at once.

PAWS UP!

Just then, I heard a noise. "**Paws up!**" a voice squeaked.

We turned around. It was Nastytail and his crew. Fortunately, they had not seen the oil gushing out of the well.

"Hey, Boss. That's Strongfur's daughter," Bones told Nastytail. "Let's hold her hostage. That will make her father obey us!"

Nastytail nodded. "Good idea," he muttered. *"I was just going to say that."*

Miceson stared at us with a menacing look. "Who do you want me to **SQUASH**, Boss?" he sneered. "Just give me the word and I'll do it!"

Then he punched a stone slab. It broke in two and landed on his paw. A monkey bit his other paw.

"Owwwwwwwww!" Miceson squeaked.

Bones giggled under his whiskers.

My cousin rolled his eyes. "What a bunch of nitwits," he scoffed. "You haven't even noticed the ruby."

Thea elbowed him to keep quiet.

But Bones perked up his ears. "Yes, legend has it that there's a giant **ruby** hidden here," he grinned. "We have to make them spill the beans, Boss."

Nastytail nodded. "Um, right. Spill the beans," he muttered. *"I was just going to say that."*

Miceson puffed up his chest. "**Do what the boss said. Spill the beansprouts or I will squash you!**" he growled.

This time, he didn't hit anything. Instead, he twirled around in a circle, punching the air. After a while, he had to sit down. He looked dizzy.

Bones giggled. The rest of us kept quiet. The **ruby** was right under our snouts. But there was no way we were going to tell these bozos.

Bones thought for a moment. "Let's threaten to mousenap Monkeyfur," he said to Nastytail. "That will get them squeaking."

Nastytail shook his head. "Yes, yes," he agreed. *"I was just going to say that."*

They grabbed Monkeyfur.

At that moment, the professor jumped up. "Leave her alone!" he commanded. "The ruby is here. Right under your **SNOUTS**."

He pointed to the well.

The rotten rodents stared at the glittering stone. Three pairs of eyes opened wide. Three jaws hit the ground. "**Jackpot!**" they shrieked with glee.

The rotten rodents stared at the glittering stone.

Oo! Eee! OOOOO!

The three scoundrels pounced on the stone like a hungry cat on a sleeping mouse.

"The ruby is so **big!**" Nastytail cried. "I wonder what it's **worth**."

Bones pulled a calculator out of his pocket. He punched in some numbers. Then he showed the total to Nastytail.

Nastytail gulped. "I'm *rich*!" he shrieked.

Just at that moment, a few drops of oil dripped out of the faucet.

Bones stared at the oil. "Boss, this is oil! There must be an oil well under this stone!" he giggled. "We won't be rich, we'll be stinking rich!"

Bones and Miceson slapped paws. "We're stinking rich! We're stinking rich!" they chanted. They were so excited. They did cartwheels around the room. They looked like two mouselets on Christmas morning.

Nastytail frowned. "I am the boss!" he roared. "I will say who is rich around here!" Then he ordered them to haul the stone away.

I noticed Monkeyfur waving to the monkeys. They had been watching us from the ceiling.

"Ooo! Ooo! Eee! Eee!" Monkeyfur yelled. In a flash, the monkeys sprang at the three villains. They began to hit them with stones and leftover avocados. I watched with envy. Those monkeys were good shots. I wondered if they ever thought

about starting a baseball team. But I didn't get a chance to ask.

Seconds later, Nastytail's two sidekicks had dropped the RUBY. "We give up! Make them stop!" the villains cried.

THE ARMY OF THE HOWLING SPIRITS

Monkeyfur shouted another order.

Immediately, the monkeys squatted in front of her. How *amazing*! They were as disciplined as a little army. She gave some fruit to the monkeys. They nibbled on it happily.

"For years, we have fed the army of the **HOWLING SPIRITS**," our friend explained. "They are the guardians of the RUBY and our precious oil well. But we do not want to use too much oil. We should not waste what nature gives us."

The professor nodded. "Monkeyfur is right," he said. "Happiness comes from

wanting only what you **need**. Too many rodents in the world today want **more** than is necessary. We are squeezing the earth as if it were a LEMON. Soon there will be no natural resources left for future generations."

I thought about what the professor had said. He was right. We needed to take care of our environment. I vowed to use only recycled paper from now on. And maybe I could use less water. I could turn off the water when I brushed my teeth. And I could take a bath every other night instead of every night. Although that last one would be tough. I love a nice hot cheddar *bubble bath*. It's a great way to escape from the rat race. Cheddar bubbles, take me away!

The earth is not a lemon to squeeze.

THE TRUE GUARDIAN OF THE RUBY

I was still dreaming about that bubble bath when I heard a loud **CRASH**. I gasped. Nastytail had smashed the RUBY with his machete!

"If I can't have it, no one can!" he sneered.

Monkeyfur burst into tears. "The RUBY is lost forever!" she groaned. But for some reason a *strange* smile crept over her face. WHY? I wondered what secret she was hiding this time.

Trap tied up the villains with his rope. They sat glumly underneath a tall tree.

Then Monkeyfur led us to the other side of the temple. "I have a surprise for you!"

she said with a wink. She pushed aside some banana leaves. They hid a narrow tunnel. At the bottom of the tunnel, I saw two yellow eyes shining. They belonged to an enormouse boa constrictor. It was guarding a SPARKLING ruby.

"Sssssssssssssssssssss!" Monkeyfur hissed.

The snake slid *obediently* toward her. I was impressed. Monkeyfur couldn't read or write, but she could speak two other languages — monkey and now snake!

The snake placed the ruby in Monkeyfur's paw. She explained that this was the real ruby. For many years, EVIL RODENTS had been trying to steal it. So the villagers came up with a plan. They would put a fake ruby inside the temple. The boa constrictor GUARDED the real ruby day and night.

Here is the real ruby!

Thea turned on her two-way radio. She put in a call to the local police. "We have captured three nasty rodents," she said. "They have been **cutting down** all of the trees in the forest. Please come and get them. **Over and out!**"

Over and out!

BE SLY LIKE A
MONKEY!

The police arrived the next morning.
Trap led them to the tall **TREE**.
But the evil rodents were gone.
Trap's rope lay on the ground in pieces.

My cousin blushed. "**OOPS**," he mumbled.
"I must have used my trick breakaway rope
by accident. It's great for practical jokes,
but not so good for catching criminals."

The police **SHOOK** their heads. "Too bad,"
the shorter officer sighed. "We'll never find
them. It's too easy to hide in this forest."

Just then, I noticed Monkeyfur giggling
under her whiskers. "Don't be so sure of that.
Follow me!" she said. I had a feeling that
Monkeyfur was up to something. But what?

We walked along the path that led to the village. That's covered with twigs. That's when we spotted a deep hole

It was a trap. Down below, Nastytail was jumping up and down in ANGER. "Get me out of here!" he shrieked.

We burst out laughing. A little bit farther, we saw Mike Miceson. He was dangling upside down from a vine. "Help!" he cried. But what about Bones? Where was Bones?

Well, we came across him soon enough. He was trapped in a wooden cage. Monkeyfur had caught every last one of them. She was one clever mouse! I was

lucky to be learning from her.

"I was just following my father's advice," Monkeyfur explained. "Be *sly* as a monkey. After all, that is how I got my name!"

THE
HEADACHE PLANT

The next day, Strongfur and the rest of the villagers, big and small, returned to their homes. They were happy to be back near the *TEMPLE OF THE RUBY OF FIRE*. They invited us to stay for a while. I was excited. Now I would have time to finish teaching Monkeyfur how to read and write.

In return, she tried to teach me how to speak to the monkeys. I guess I wasn't very good, though. The monkeys laughed and laughed when I practiced. Trap and Thea joined them. "Face it, Gerry Berry, you just can't squeak their language," my cousin smirked.

Finally, it was time to leave.

I started to pack my bags, but my head was pounding. I had a terrible headache. "I'm sorry, Geronimo. I seem to have lost the FIRST-AID KIT," said the professor.

I sighed. Headaches are no fun.

I noticed Warmfur watching me. She stood up. "I can fix your head," she said. She ran away into the woods. Warmfur must have thought *she* was giving me a headache.

But she returned a few minutes later. She was carrying a little plant. The leaves were shaped like hearts. Warmfur GROUND UP the leaves into a juice.

"Drink," she ordered, giving me the juice. So I did. I mean, I didn't want to insult her. But I was nervous. What if the juice made my tail fall off? What if I sprouted wings? I closed my eyes. *Don't panic,* I told myself. It didn't work. I opened my eyes. I couldn't put my paw on it, but something was missing. I wiggled my tail. I waved my paws. Then I felt my head. Now I knew what was missing. My headache was gone!

Warmfur smiled. "This isn't magic," she said. "It is science. We call this the headache plant."

Soon the professor and Warmfur were chatting away about SCIENCE and plants. They were like two old friends.

I Love Every Tree.
I Love Every
Flower.

On the flight home, Benjamin snuggled next to me. He was filled with questions about the Amazon forest. He asked me about the animals who lived there. He asked me about the plants. I told him that many of the plants and animals in the forest are **ENDANGERED**. Pollution was slowly killing them off. We were losing some of the earth's most amazing treasures.

Benjamin shook his head sadly. "That is awful, Uncle," he said. He pulled out his notebook. Then he wrote this poem about nature.

I LOVE EVERY TREE.
I LOVE EVERY FLOWER.

I love every tree. I love every flower.

I love everything in nature,

every minute, every hour.

Clear and crystal waters,

stars that shine way high above,

rich green forests filled with creatures,

that is what I love!

A LIVING PRESENT!

The next morning, I was happy to be back at work. Don't get me wrong, I loved the rain forest. But I missed *The Rodent's Gazette.* Plus, I wasn't crazy about sleeping in the forest. I missed my comfy cozy bed. And then there was my mega **HUGE** fridge . . .

I was thinking about my favorite cheeses when Benjamin burst into my office.

"Look, Uncle! I brought you a surprise," he squeaked. "It's an avocado **pit**. You can

1. Take an avocado pit and stick four toothpicks in it about halfway.

2. Fill a glass with water. Put the pit in the water so that half the pit is submerged and the other half is above the waterline. Change the water frequently.

grow it into a plant. I wanted to give you something living."

He put the glass on my desk. I gave him a hug. Isn't my nephew  the sweetest mouse in the world?

Now he grabbed my paw. "Uncle, guess what? My teacher wants to know if you will come to our school. You could tell everyone about our ADVENTURES in the Amazon," he said. "Oh, can you, Uncle? Pretty please with a cheddar ball on top?"

I grinned. How could I say no to such an adorable rodent?

3. When small roots have formed, plant the pit in a pot with good soil. Water it frequently so that the soil is always slightly damp.

WHAT IS THE
AMAZON FOREST?

On Monday, I went to school with Benjamin. His friends asked lots of questions. I squeaked and squeaked until I was blue in the face. Well, I guess I didn't really turn blue. After all, have you ever seen a blue mouse?????

What is the Amazon?
It's a region around the Amazon River. It's huge: more than two million square miles. That's ten times the size of Texas!

It's covered with dense forest, called rain forest, because it rains a lot. The air is always very humid. It's hot; the temperature fluctuates between 77 and 95 degrees Fahrenheit all year round.

Do the Yanomami really live in the Amazon forest?
Yes. They grow sweet potatoes, bananas, and gather mushrooms, berries, and honey. They eat monkeys,

tapirs, and even insects. They hunt using bows and arrows. They also use blowpipes, which are hollow tubes that tiny arrows are blown through. (Sometimes the arrows are dipped in a poison called curare.) The Yanomami are good fisherman. They live in huts made out of leaves and sleep in braided hammocks.

What animals live in the Amazon forest?

Some very strange animals like a bird-eating spider (8 inches long); the birdwing butterfly, the largest in the

Who will save the Amazon forest?

world (12-inch wingspan); and carnivorous ants, poisonous frogs, and piranhas (fish that have razor-sharp teeth). Even the slowest animal in the world, the sloth, lives there.

What plants grow in the Amazon forest?
Strange plants grow there, like the giant rafflesia, whose flower is three feet wide and weighs 22 pounds. The pitcher plant is a carnivorous plant that eats insects.

Many species are even more mysterious, and scientists hope that these Amazon plants will be the source to obtain remedies for some serious diseases.

What does the Amazon forest resemble?
A building with many floors. The tallest trees form the canopy, up to one hundred feet above the earth, where birds and monkeys live.

The Amazon forest is a precious treasure
for everyone in the world, and everyone must
take the responsibility of saving it.

Underneath the canopy is the intermediate level, around fifty feet above the earth, where cats, bats, and snakes live.

Below that is the ground, dark and humid, where jaguars, serpents, and spiders live.

Why is the forest in danger?

Today, trees are cut down to create space for fields to be cultivated and to harvest precious woods. Often, the trees are cut down illegally.

The destruction of the forest puts in danger all the species of plants and animals that live there. Many species run the risk of becoming extinct, which means they may disappear forever.

Why is the forest important?

The Amazon plants help to maintain the equilibrium of the planet.

The earth is surrounded by atmosphere, formed by many gases, including oxygen, which is used for breathing.

Even carbon dioxide is present in the atmosphere. If there is too much, the earth gets hot. This phenomenon is called the greenhouse effect, and it is dangerous. The big forests absorb the carbon dioxide in the air and help to combat the greenhouse effect.

ANIMALS IN THE AMAZON FOREST

1. Montezuma oropendula bird nests
2. Blue-and-gold macaw
3. Silver marmoset monkeys
4. Wedge-capped capuchin monkey
5. Razor-back
6. Indian grass snake
7. Ibis
8. Helena butterfly
9. Anaconda
10. Capybara
11. Jaguar
12. Leaf-cutting ant
13. Opossum
14. Howler monkey
15. Geoffrey marmoset
16. Sloth
17. Toucan
18. Giant otter
19. Tapir
20. Brazilian giant black spider
21. Boa constrictor
22. Tortoise

ABOUT THE AUTHOR

Born in New Mouse City, Mouse Island, Geronimo Stilton is Rattus Emeritus of Mousomorphic Literature and of Neo-Ratonic Comparative Philosophy. For the past twenty years, he has been running *The Rodent's Gazette*, New Mouse City's most widely read daily newspaper.

Stilton was awarded the Ratitzer Prize for his scoop on *The Curse of the Cheese Pyramid*. He has also received the Andersen 2000 Prize for Personality of the Year. One of his best-sellers won the 2002 eBook Award for world's best ratlings' electronic book. His works have been published all over the globe.

In his spare time, Mr. Stilton collects antique cheese rinds and plays golf. But what he most enjoys is telling stories to his nephew Benjamin.

Want to read my next adventure?
It's sure to be a fur-raising experience!

THE MONA MOUSA CODE

Do you like solving mysteries? I do! So
when my sister, Thea, heard that there was
a secret hidden in Mouse Island's most
famouse painting, the *Mona Mousa*, I knew
we had to crack the code! We began to
investigate, and soon we were following a
trail of clues that led us below the streets of
New Mouse City. There we made the most
fabumouse discovery. . . .

Don't miss any of my other fabumouse adventures!

#1 Lost Treasure of the Emerald Eye
#2 The Curse of the Cheese Pyramid
#3 Cat and Mouse in a Haunted House
#4 I'm Too Fond of My Fur!
#5 Four Mice Deep in the Jungle
#6 Paws Off, Cheddarface!
#7 Red Pizzas for a Blue Count
#8 Attack of the Bandit Cats
#9 A Fabumouse Vacation for Geronimo
#10 All Because of a Cup of Coffee
#11 It's Halloween, You 'Fraidy Mouse!
#12 Merry Christmas, Geronimo!
#13 The Phantom of the Subway
#14 The Temple of the Ruby of Fire
#15 The Mona Mousa Code
#16 A Cheese-Colored Camper
#17 Watch Your Whiskers, Stilton!
#18 Shipwreck on the Pirate Islands
#19 My Name is Stilton, Geronimo Stilton
#20 Surf's Up, Geronimo!
#21 The Wild, Wild West
#22 The Secret of Cacklefur Castle
#23 Valentine's Day Disaster
#24 Field Trip to Niagara Falls

#25 The Search for Sunken Treasure
#26 The Mummy With No Name
#27 The Christmas Toy Factory
#28 Wedding Crasher
#29 Down and Out Down Under
#30 The Mouse Island Marathon
#31 The Mysterious Cheese Thief
#32 Valley of the Giant Skeletons
#33 Geronimo and the Gold Medal Mystery
#34 Geronimo Stilton, Secret Agent
#35 A Very Merry Christmas
#36 Geronimo's Valentine
#37 The Race Across America
#38 A Fabumouse School Adventure
#39 Singing Sensation
#40 The Karate Mouse
#41 Mighty Mount Kilimanjaro
#42 The Peculiar Pumpkin Thief
#43 I'm Not a Supermouse!
#44 The Giant Diamond Robbery
#45 The Haunted Castle
A Christmas Tale
Christmas Catastrophe

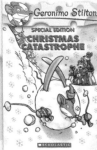

Be sure to check out these very special editions!

THE KINGDOM OF FANTASY

THE QUEST FOR PARADISE:
THE RETURN TO THE KINGDOM OF FANTASY

And look for this series about my friend Creepella von Cacklefur!

#1 THE THIRTEEN GHOSTS

#2 MEET ME IN HORRORWOOD

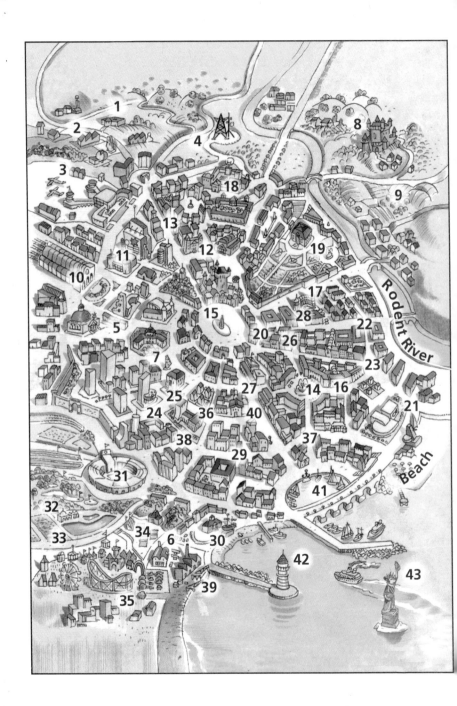

Map of New Mouse City

1. Industrial Zone
2. Cheese Factories
3. Angorat International Airport
4. WRAT Radio and Television Station
5. Cheese Market
6. Fish Market
7. Town Hall
8. Snotnose Castle
9. The Seven Hills of Mouse Island
10. Mouse Central Station
11. Trade Center
12. Movie Theater
13. Gym
14. Catnegie Hall
15. Singing Stone Plaza
16. The Gouda Theater
17. Grand Hotel
18. Mouse General Hospital
19. Botanical Gardens
20. Cheap Junk for Less (Trap's store)
21. Parking Lot
22. Mouseum of Modern Art
23. University and Library
24. *The Daily Rat*
25. *The Rodent's Gazette*
26. Trap's House
27. Fashion District
28. The Mouse House Restaurant
29. Environmental Protection Center
30. Harbor Office
31. Mousidon Square Garden
32. Golf Course
33. Swimming Pool
34. Blushing Meadow Tennis Courts
35. Curlyfur Island Amusement Park
36. Geronimo's House
37. New Mouse City Historic District
38. Public Library
39. Shipyard
40. Thea's House
41. New Mouse Harbor
42. Luna Lighthouse
43. The Statue of Liberty

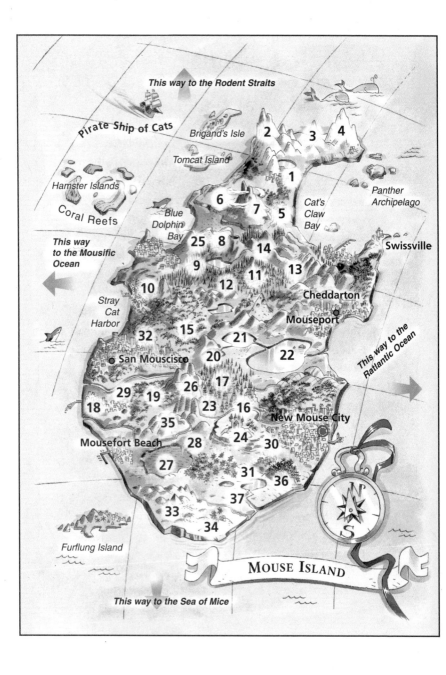

Map of Mouse Island

1. Big Ice Lake
2. Frozen Fur Peak
3. Slipperyslopes Glacier
4. Coldcreeps Peak
5. Ratzikistan
6. Transratania
7. Mount Vamp
8. Roastedrat Volcano
9. Brimstone Lake
10. Poopedcat Pass
11. Stinko Peak
12. Dark Forest
13. Vain Vampires Valley
14. Goose Bumps Gorge
15. The Shadow Line Pass
16. Penny Pincher Lodge
17. Nature Reserve Park
18. Las Ratayas Marinas
19. Fossil Forest
20. Lake Lake
21. Lake Lake Lake
22. Lake Lakelakelake
23. Cheddar Crag
24. Cannycat Castle
25. Valley of the Giant Sequoia
26. Cheddar Springs
27. Sulfurous Swamp
28. Old Reliable Geyser
29. Vole Vail
30. Ravingrat Ravine
31. Gnat Marshes
32. Munster Highlands
33. Mousehara Desert
34. Oasis of the Sweaty Camel
35. Cabbagehead Hill
36. Rattytrap Jungle
37. Rio Mosquito

THE RODENT'S GAZETTE

1. **Main Entrance**

2. **Printing presses** (where the books and newspaper are printed)

3. **Accounts department**

4. **Editorial room** (where the editors, illustrators, and designers work)

5. **Geronimo Stilton's office**

6. **Storage space for Geronimo's books**

If you like my brother's books, you'll love mine!

THEA STILTON AND THE DRAGON'S CODE

THEA STILTON AND THE MOUNTAIN OF FIRE

THEA STILTON AND THE GHOST OF THE SHIPWRECK

THEA STILTON AND THE SECRET CITY

THEA STILTON AND THE MYSTERY IN PARIS

THEA STILTON AND THE CHERRY BLOSSOM ADVENTURE

THEA STILTON AND THE STAR CASTAWAYS

Dear mouse friends,
Thanks for reading, and farewell
till the next book.
It'll be another whisker-licking-good
adventure, and that's a promise!

Geronimo Stilton